SPARKS

OTHER DELL YEARLING BOOKS
YOU WILL ENJOY

SPARKS

Graham McNamee

A Dell Yearling Book

Big thanks to Phyllis Naylor for her kindness and the support of the
PEN/Phyllis Naylor Working Writer Fellowship. A giant thank-you hug goes
out to W.L.

Published by
Dell Yearling
an imprint of
Random House Children's Books
a division of Random House, Inc.
New York

Visit us on the Web! www.randomhouse.com/kids

Educators and librarians, for a variety of teaching tools, visit us
at www.randomhouse.com/teachers

ISBN: 0-440-41847-X

Reprinted by arrangement with Wendy Lamb Books

Printed in the United States of America

December 2003

10 9 8 7 6 5 4 3 2

OPM

For Tasha Bryer,
my first reader and best chum

My mouse died yesterday. He was white with pink eyes and he once ate a whole grape in one sitting. I remember thinking how impossible it was for him to finish that grape—I mean it was half the size of his head. It took him ten minutes. Then he washed up for ten minutes. Then he went to sleep. I loved watching him, even when his cage smelled bad. His name was Psycho, named after a movie my parents won't let me see.

This morning at breakfast I tell Mom the grape-eating story.

"It would be like me eating a whole watermelon," I say.

My sister, Christie, flicks a Froot Loop at me from across the table. It hits me in the forehead and makes me blink. She has good aim.

"I'd pay to see that," Christie says.

She really bugs me. She once stuck an apple seed so deep into my ear, I had to go to the emergency room. Every time she comes near me I blink like she's going to hit me, which she sometimes does.

But she did give me one of her jewelry boxes to bury Psycho in. It had blue velvet lining. He's buried in the backyard, under the tree for shade.

I look down at my cereal. The Froot Loop landed in my Frosted Flakes. It looks lost, a Loop all alone in the middle of all those Flakes.

"Eat up, Melonhead," Christie tells me.

"Someday I'm going to eat a whole watermelon. Then you'll be sorry," I say. But even before I finish saying it I hear how stupid that sounds. Inside my head it sounded a lot better, like something the President might say.

She shakes her head. "Just keep those fingers jammed up your nose so your brain doesn't leak out."

Christie's a genius. She always knows what to say.

Last night, Dad told me how mice only live a year or two. I got Psycho over a year ago for my ninth birthday. If I'd known he was going to die, I would have given him an extra raisin for breakfast.

It was weird trying to fall asleep last night without the squeaking of Psycho's exercise wheel spinning. He probably ran a thousand miles inside that cage. I kept waking up thinking I heard his wheel.

But I must have been dreaming.

By the time I think about all this stuff, my cereal

2

has sunk. It's way too soggy to eat now. Only the Loop is still floating.

Mom takes my bowl away.

"Countdown," she says. "Five minutes and counting."

Every morning there's the countdown for the school bus. On TV they have countdowns for the space shuttle, or for when a bomb's going to go off.

But when I leave the house there's never a space shuttle at the curb, just the bus waiting for me to get on before it explodes.

2

At home, only Christie shouts at me. At school, everybody takes turns.

Mr. Retardo, they call me. Or Brain-Dead. They're always coming up with new ones.

My real name is Todd, but the only people who seem to know that are my teacher, Mr. Blaylock, and Eva, who used to be my best friend.

Lately, they call me Gump. Like that guy in the movie *Forrest Gump*. He wasn't too smart, and he looked like somebody put a bowl on his head to give him a haircut, so the bottom half is buzzed short and the top half sticks up. They call me that because my dad makes me get scalped all the time. I get a crew cut once a month, like I'm in the army or something. He gets the same cut and says that's the kind of haircut you can salute. I don't know what that means. All

4

I know is if we get separated they'll know we belong together because of our hair.

The other reason they call me Gump is because I spent most of last year in the Special Needs class. *Special Needs* means I'm kind of a slow learner. It doesn't mean I'm a Basket Case or a Drooling Idiot—other names they call me.

But this year I'm back in the regular class for a "trial period" to see if I can make it in the real fifth grade. The big leagues.

How am I doing?

Bad. Real bad.

"Take your time, Todd," Mr. Blaylock tells me. "There's all the time in the world."

What does he mean? If I wait long enough, will the answer come to me? I've tried that. Nothing ever comes. I asked Mom if maybe she dropped me on my head by accident when I was a baby.

"No," she said. "Why would I do that?"

"I don't know. Maybe you were throwing me in the air and had to go answer the phone."

She gave me the look that means I'm being silly.

Last week when we had to show our science projects, mine was the only one that didn't work. Mr. Blaylock gave me electricity for my project. Bad idea.

I followed all the instructions in the science workbook. But when I finished, my project looked nothing like the picture in the book. I still have no idea where I went wrong.

The little red lightbulb that was supposed to light

up stayed dark. It didn't even blink for a second. Not a spark. It's like I killed electricity. It took a million years to invent and now it was dead because I touched it.

Science was easier in Special Needs. All we had to do there was grow different kinds of seeds in Styrofoam cups.

I'm walking down the hall to class, thinking about that tiny plant I made last year, when I see Eva coming toward me.

She sat beside me in Special Needs last year, and I used to help her out with stuff in class. On the last day of school she shared the radish she had grown with me. We both ended up spitting it out. Burned my tongue. But it was great.

"Todd," she says. "Look what I've got!"

Eva digs into her jacket pocket and comes out with a big bunch of Kleenex all balled up.

"Wow!" I say. "Kleenex."

She punches me on the shoulder. "Goofball! There's something inside the Kleenex."

She unfolds it and then holds her hand out to show me a bunch of seashells.

"You went to the beach?" I ask.

"On Sunday. My dad said it's Indian summer right now, so it wasn't cold or anything. I called to get you to come, but your mom said you were out somewhere."

The truth is, I wasn't really out somewhere. When

Eva phoned, I was just lying on the couch reading an X-Men comic. I had to beg Mom to tell Eva I wasn't home. But Mom said she wasn't going to lie. So I had to put my shoes on and stand outside the front door before Mom would tell Eva I was out. When I came back in Mom just shook her head at me.

I've been hiding out from Eva since school started up again. We spent the summer together, but now I'm back in the regular class with the normal kids. I'm trying to act intelligent so I won't be Mr. Retardo anymore. No more Gump. No more Brain-Dead.

Just Todd.

Eva looks at her feet. "I still got sand in my shoes," she says.

Then, right in the middle of the hall, she takes off her left shoe and shakes half the beach out of her sneaker. I hope nobody's watching.

"Put your shoe back on. Everybody's gonna think you're a nutcase." I kind of bark the words, and she seems shocked for a second before she slips her sneaker back on.

I look around, but nobody's in sight.

Eva kicks at the sand she poured out like she's trying to rub it away into the floor.

"Do you want to look at my shells?" she asks, holding the Kleenex ball out to me.

"I can't," I say. "I have to get to class. I'll see you around sometime."

Then I walk away down the hall. I look back as I go into the classroom and see Eva standing where I left her, like she's frozen there.

3

I sit down at my desk and stare at the blank blackboard, trying not to think about Eva. But she won't get out of my head.

It feels like my breakfast flakes have squeezed together into a rock inside my stomach. A cold rock. I hate barking at her like that, but she has to know I can't hang around with her anymore. People will think I'm still Brain-Dead.

Why did she have to show me that stupid ball of Kleenex? Why did she have to pour all that stupid sand on the stupid floor? And why does she have to be so nice?

Mr. Blaylock walks into the room, blocking my view of the board. He is a big man. Not fat big, but *big* big. He looks like the Incredible Hulk, except in a suit. And he's got brown skin instead of green.

The first week of school, I kept expecting him to get me in a headlock whenever he stood by my desk to see how I was doing. One time he was helping me fix a math problem I was working on, and it was like his shadow blocked out all the light in the room. He took my pencil and it looked like a toothpick in his hand. Like it shrank when he touched it.

"You started out all right," he said. He didn't sound like the Hulk, who only ever roared. "But right here you made a wrong turn."

I'm always making wrong turns.

Now, at his desk, Mr. Blaylock opens his briefcase.

"Here are your science tests back. There are two things we have to clear up. Number one—Venezuela is not one of the nine planets, it's a country in South America. Number two—there were no dinosaurs roaming the earth in 100 B.C. That was the time of the Roman empire, and I don't remember Caesar wrestling any T. rexes."

I can feel my face go red. That was one of my answers, the one about the dinosaurs.

"Come up when your name is called."

Mr. Blaylock hands out the tests, making comments to each student like "You can do better" and "You're showing improvement."

When I go up all I get is silence. I grab my paper and run back to my desk. There are so many red marks on my test. I turn it facedown on my desk, but you can still see all the red X's where the marker soaked right through the paper. It looks like someone had a nosebleed on it.

When I'm sure nobody's looking I flip it over. At the bottom is written SEE ME AFTER SCHOOL.

There's a big fat D- beside my name at the top, like that's going to be my grade forever so they might as well just add it onto my name.

From behind me in the next row over, someone coughs. Only they're not really coughing, they're just faking a cough, and under their breath they say, "Retard."

Cough—"Retard."

I peek back and see that it's Zero who's doing that. He's been looking over my shoulder at my D-. Now he sticks his finger up his nose and makes a face like a Drooling Idiot.

Jackie Williams goes up when her name is called.

"Perfect as always," Mr. B. tells her as he hands back her test.

Jackie is a genius. Everything she does gets an A+. She must have read the whole library. She even talks in sentences and paragraphs, with commas and everything.

She sits at the desk on my right, so I can see her paper.

A++, it says at the top. That's impossible. You would have to discover a new country or something to get an A++. Or know what longitude is.

Jackie even looks perfect. She has dark brown hair the exact same color as her skin. Her hair is parted in the middle, combed into rows and braided so every hair is exactly where it's supposed to be. I'm sure she's never had a cavity or had an apple seed stuck in her ear.

"Okay now," Mr. Blaylock says. "Math is the name of the game this hour."

There are groans from the class.

Mr. B. smiles. "Hey, fractions are my favorite too."

$$\frac{11}{2} \times \frac{22}{12} \div \frac{1}{2}$$

There's no escape. When the bell rings to end the day I think about making a break for it and trying to sneak out with the crowd. But that's no good. I'd have to come back tomorrow. I can't sneak out of my whole life.

SEE ME AFTER SCHOOL.

That's an order. I sit frozen at my desk as the other kids leave.

While the teacher's back is turned, Zero points at me and laughs silently as he's leaving. Zero isn't his real name—his mother didn't name him that. His real name is Ronald. He got nicknamed Zero because that's how smart he is. Zero. Whoever thought that up is probably assassinated now. But I'd take it over Mr. Retardo any day.

Zero even failed two grades, but he never got sent to Special Needs like me. He's just as dumb as I am, he just hides it better.

"Todd," Mr. Blaylock says in his low voice that makes my knees shake. "How do you like your new class?"

What do I say? What's the right answer?

"Yes," I say. "I mean, I really like it."

He looks so huge sitting there. I must look like a bug to him, like a beetle. No, that's too big—more like an ant.

"What's your favorite subject?"

That's like asking me what's my favorite fraction. There is no good subject. They're all out to get me.

I point to the aquarium on the counter by the wall.

"I like the frogs and sala . . . salamanders in the aquarium."

Mr. Blaylock smiles like I said something right. He gets up and goes to the counter, waving me over. I get tangled in my chair getting up and it squeals way too loud.

Great, now he's going to think I can't even stand without screwing up.

He bends down and looks in at the little land-scape behind the glass. There's a frog the size of a quarter stuck to the glass inside. You can see its belly breathing in and out. Mr. Blaylock puts his finger on the outside of the glass where the frog is. I'm surprised it doesn't jump away. It doesn't even notice that thick finger, which could crush it easy.

"It's actually called a terrarium. Aquariums are filled with water for fish. Terrariums are for amphibians and reptiles," he tells me. "I got my first one when I was ten. They're perfect miniature worlds. How many frogs do we have in there now?"

"Four," I say. "And a half."

His big black eyes focus on me. "How do you get half a frog?"

"One died behind the blue rock there."

He squints in through the side to see the back of the blue rock.

"Hmmm. Right you are," he says. "That little guy's not looking too happy."

"I had a mouse who died," I tell him.

"Sorry to hear that."

Mr. Blaylock lifts the top off the aquarium—I mean terrarium—and picks the dead frog out, using a paper towel.

He starts folding the towel around the frog.

"Todd, I think you would be learning a lot more in the Special Needs class. What do you think?"

Special Needs. The Brain-Dead Class. The Drooling Idiots.

"I just got out of that class. Please, I don't want to go back there. I'll do better."

He keeps folding the paper towel like he's making an envelope or something. You would think hands that big could only crush stuff, not fold so neat.

"I can make it," I tell him. "I swear I can. Just give me another chance."

He stops making the little paper-towel coffin for the frog and looks me in the eye.

"I'll tell you what. The first report cards come out at the end of October, four weeks from now. We'll see how things look by then. Deal?"

Four weeks! That's like a Mission Impossible! I've spent my whole life being an idiot. What can I do in four weeks?

"Deal," I say. What choice do I have?

"Give it your best shot." He smiles and puts his giant hand on my shoulder.

Mr. Blaylock holds the wrapped-up frog in his other hand, gentle as if it was still alive and he didn't want to scare it.

4

When I stop in the hallway to zip up my backpack, I hear laughter coming from room 204. That's the room I spent last year in.

"Harvey, you've got to use soap to get that out," Miss Wisswell says.

I miss her. She was my best teacher ever. She never scared me.

"It's all dried and hard," Harvey says.

"Well, what were you doing putting orange paint in your hair?" Miss Wisswell asks.

"Orangutans have orange hair."

"Harvey, are you an orangutan?"

There's this long silence. Then he says, "No. I guess not."

I can hear Miss Wisswell talking to some of the other kids. "Eva, can you rinse off those brushes?"

I get all nervous when I hear Eva's name. I feel bad enough already, I don't want to have to yell at her again. So I hurry and wait out front for Mom to come pick me up.

Harvey's been crazy about orangutans ever since we went on that field trip to the Metro Zoo last year and one of those orange monkeys pressed its lips to the glass of its cage. Harvey fell in love with it.

That was a great trip. Eva found a peacock feather and we watched a lion go to the bathroom. That was amazing—the feather, I mean. Miss Wisswell told us how the male peacock fans out all those bright feathers to show off. Eva let me hold the feather and then when I gave it back she held my hand for a while, for no reason. Which was nice, until Harvey started staring and I had to shake her off.

I wouldn't say Eva is slow, even if maybe she is. She's not like Harvey, though. Harvey's really hyper. He bounces all the time until you get dizzy watching him. When he's supposed to be standing still he jumps in place like the floor's really hot or something. When he's sitting down his legs are pumping like he's pedaling a bike. Even Miss Wisswell has to shout at him sometimes to slow him down.

But Eva's different. Her problem is, when she gets a wrong answer in math or anything and the teacher shows her where she went wrong, Eva will do the whole thing over and make the exact same mistake. She does this a million times over. Miss Wisswell called her stubborn.

That's Eva. She might get the wrong answer sometimes, but she never gives up. She's like the Terminator that way.

She'll be back.

5

For homework tonight I'm supposed to read two chapters from *Charlotte's Web*. Twelve pages. That will take me all week. What am I, a professor?

"Grow a brain," the kids in class are always telling me, like it's an easy thing. It's not like that radish we grew last year in Special Needs. You can't just water your brain and put it in the window to get some sun.

Grow a brain. Fast. That's my Mission Impossible.

I lie back in bed, opening the book wide and cracking its spine. I like the way books have spines, so I can crack them and torture the books the way they torture me.

Page one. I'm okay for the first three paragraphs, but then I start spacing out.

It's a few minutes later when I snort awake with

Charlotte's Web open on my face. I don't even remember falling asleep. This reading stuff can really knock you out.

I gotta concentrate! Sitting up, I knock on my head like I'm trying to see if anybody's home. No answer.

I once saw this thing on TV where a bald guy was standing on his head and reading a book at the same time. Mom was watching the show. She said Baldy was doing yoga, some kind of exercise where you don't move. Mom does yoga too. She can put her foot behind her head. It's pretty freaky. But she said it clears the mind when you stand on your head. I guess all your blood puddles in your brain and it just sort of floats there.

I tried standing on my head before, but I kept falling over and crashing into stuff. So I'll try the next-best thing.

Leaning out over the edge of my bed, I let my arms hang down, holding *Charlotte's Web*. The edge of the bed is right in the middle of my gut, and the way my head hangs over I can feel the blood rushing to it. This has got to boost my brainpower. It's like when Dad fires up the barbecue by squirting a bunch of lighter fluid on the coals. Except I'm squirting blood on my brain to light it on fire.

I think it's working. I get through a whole page without getting lost. So I lean out a bit farther. My heartbeat sounds louder now, because I guess all the blood is rushing past my ears, and my head feels like it's swelling up like a balloon. I'm getting dizzy and the words are going all blurry.

"Todd? What are you doing?" That's Mom's voice, but I'm leaning over so far and my head's so fuzzy that I can't tell where her voice is coming from or which way is up. I stare at the floor, then under my bed, wondering what she'd be doing down there.

"Mom?"

Right then I hang out a half inch too far and crash to the floor. My hands and *Charlotte* break the fall. I'm stunned for a second, and when I try to sit up it feels like I've been spinning in circles.

Mom crouches down beside me. "Well, there goes another dent in your head," she says. "Your skull has more craters than the moon."

"I was reading," I say, trying to explain.

"Upside down?"

"Yeah. So there'd be more blood in my brain. It's like yoga."

"You're not supposed to land on your head doing yoga."

Mom feels around in my hair to make sure there's no cracks in my skull. I liked it better when we used to read books together and she was right there when something needed explaining.

"I'm trying to get smarter," I say.

"That's good. But banging your head isn't the best way to go about it."

"Guess not," I agree. And she's right, that bang knocked everything I just read out of my head.

It's safer to watch TV.

Dad and me are sitting on the couch, watching a movie where a plane crashes on a deserted island and the survivors have to live off of what they can hunt and fish. Right now they're barbecuing a seven-foot python.

Me, I'm eating ketchup-flavored potato chips. Dad's working his way through a bowl of miniature carrots. He must eat a couple dozen of those things a day—not because they're healthy, because he just needs to be doing something with his hands.

See, he quit smoking for the millionth time nine days ago. Dad used to be a two-pack-a-day guy. When we look at old photos in the family album, Dad's always kind of blurry because he's hidden behind a fog of cigarette smoke. He's gone from being a chain-smoker to a chain-carrot-eater.

"I saw on this science show," I tell him, "how there was this guy who was crazy about being healthy. And so he ate hundreds of carrots a week. Real carrots, the big ones. And he ate so many he started turning orange."

Dad snorts. "No way."

"It's true. It was on TV—the Learning Channel."

That's the thing about being slow, even when you're right nobody believes you. But I'm not giving up. "There's this ingredient in carrots that makes them orange. So—"

"Beta-carotene," Dad says.

"Who?"

"That's the thing in carrots that gives them their color."

"Right. That's it," I tell him. "Beeta . . . canateen. Whatever. That's the stuff."

"So you're afraid your old man's going to turn orange?"

I shrug. "Well, you don't want people making fun of you. Like remember that time my hand turned green and when I went to school they thought I was radioactive."

That was back when Dad was making his own beer in the basement and he was creating a special St. Patrick's Day brew. So he added a bunch of green dye, because green is Irish people's favorite color and St. Patrick is Irish. I was helping pour the dye, only the jug was too heavy and I got more dye on me than in the brew.

Dad laughs. "That was just food coloring. And we managed to scrub it off you after a couple of days."

"Yeah."

Dad points at me with one of his midget carrots. "Keep an eye on me. If I start changing colors I'll switch to eating celery."

I finish the ketchup chips and lick my fingers clean. Under the coffee table I spot my inflatable globe that I was using yesterday to study geography. It's about the size of a basketball when it's blown up. I spin the globe on one finger but it keeps sliding off.

"Todd," Mom calls from the kitchen. "Phone!"

"Who is it?" I holler back.

"Eva."

The globe slides off my finger and bounces off the table, rolling beside the TV. I thought after today in the hall and me barking at her, Eva would stay a million miles away. But I forgot what a Terminator she is.

I go over and poke my head in the kitchen. "Mom," I whisper.

"What?" she says, covering the talking end of the phone with her hand.

"I can't talk to her. Tell her I'm outside some-where."

"Why?" Mom wants to know.

"Just because."

"I won't lie, Todd."

"Um, how about if I just go stand outside like last time? Please? *Please?*"

Mom shakes her head like she's disappointed.

I know. I'm a rotten kid.

"This is the last time!" she tells me.

I stand out front in my socks, shivering in the night wind until it's safe to come back in again.

Christie took my seat while I was gone. She's eating a peanut butter and banana sandwich. I hate peanut butter ever since she tried to smother me with one of those sandwiches and it got all up my nose and everything.

I missed the end of the plane crash movie and Dad's gone upstairs, so I can't ask him what happened.

I have to ask Christie. "Did you see if they got rescued off the island?"

"Everybody except a little snotty kid named Todd," Christie says. "You're such a creep."

"Hey, what are you bugging me for? I didn't do nothing."

"Right. I don't know why Eva even tries. She doesn't have to scrape the bottom of the barrel for friends like you."

Christie's only two years older than me, but she's a lot bigger. She's in junior high now. When she was still in my school she acted like she didn't know me. Because I say stupid things and look like an idiot, Christie says. Those are good reasons, I guess.

The thing is, she's like one of those Formula One racing cars speeding to the finish line. The way Christie sees it, I'm in her way, slowing her down.

"You got a zit on your nose," I tell Christie. It's not true, but I figure it's the fastest way to get my seat back.

"You *are* a zit," she says as she shoves past me. Down the hall the bathroom door slams behind her.

I grab the globe and take my place on the couch

again. But now the news is on and the news is so boring. Something's always wrong somewhere, they just change the names around.

I turn the globe in my lap, looking for deserted islands.

Mom comes and sits beside me, stirring her yogurt.

"So, how come you won't talk to Eva anymore? I thought she was your best friend."

I shrug. "I don't know."

Mom nudges me. "Come on."

"It's just that I'm not in her class anymore. Everybody will think I'm still, you know, Brain-Dead."

Mom frowns at me. "You were *never* brain-dead. That's a horrible thing to say. Do the kids call you that?"

"Doesn't matter."

"You just learn at a different speed. That's all. Like Eva," Mom says.

"But I'm not like Eva anymore. I'm in the real fifth grade with the normal kids. This is the big leagues, Mom. I don't want to go back."

She licks her spoon clean. Until a year ago, I always thought yogurt was just melted ice cream. But then I tasted some and it was more like ice cream someone poured vinegar into and then left in the sun for a week.

"You can still be friends," she tells me. Mom is supersmart—she went to college and everything. But sometimes she just doesn't get it.

On the globe I find a tiny little island with no name on it, right in the middle of nowhere in the Pacific Ocean.

I can't talk to Eva anymore, and we can't hang out like we used to. But still, if I had to crash-land in the middle of nowhere with anybody, it would be Eva.

6

"Hey, Gump!"

I hear the voice calling behind me and I freeze.

"Hey, Gump!" Zero comes up beside me. "You dropped something," he says, shoving the books I'm holding out of my hands.

Math Explorer and *Who Invented It?* go crashing to the floor.

"Gump," he says. "Gump the chump."

Just what I need, a new name.

"Think I'll bump Gump the chump," Zero says, shoving me against the wall.

Great. Now he's going to kill me and rhyme at the same time.

I lean on the wall, holding my breath. There's no use running. The best thing to do is just play dead and hope he'll go away. Or does that only work with bears?

"Think I'll lump and bump Gump the chump."

"Boys," an adult voice says. It's the vice principal. "Don't loiter in the halls. Get to class."

Saved! I don't know what *loiter* means. It must have something to do with getting beat up.

Whatever. I grab my books off the floor and hurry to class.

Today we start with history. We're doing the Civil War. Mr. Blaylock is talking about famous battles of the war.

"Who can tell me the name of the general who led the Confederates in the battle for the Shenandoah Valley?"

I slouch over and stare at my desktop, trying to be invisible. Usually it works. But—

"Todd?" Mr. B. says. "Any ideas?"

I squint and squeeze my head with my hand to force out the answer.

"Um, Stonewall?" I mumble.

"Stonewall Jackson. Good, Todd."

Wow. I got it right, even if it was by accident. That's the only Civil War name I know, and the only reason I remember it is because it sounds like a wrestler's name. *Stonewall.* You can almost see that general jumping off the top rope for a flying body slam.

Like my dad says, even a busted clock is right two

times a day. Still, it's great to get a nod from Mr. Blaylock.

When the battle for the Shenandoah Valley ends we go on to math. Math hour goes on forever, like it's multiplying itself. I wish it would divide itself so it would be over already. Jackie Williams always has the answer before anybody else. She doesn't even write it down, she does it in her head. Sometimes she catches me staring at her and she looks at me like I'm a bug.

Then comes geography, where Mr. B. starts talking about longitude and latitude. They're these lines on maps that you can't see in the real world. They crisscross the planet, sort of like a game of tic-tac-toe, but without the X's and O's.

Before the final bell sounds, just when I think I'm going to get out of here alive, Mr. B. tells us there's a quiz tomorrow. *Quiz*—that word is like an icicle stabbed in my heart.

"We're going to test your knowledge of geography, my friends," Mr. B. says. "Know your states and capitals, your lakes and rivers. Your north, south, east, and west."

I'm going to have to do more with my globe tonight than dribble it. I'm going to have to memorize it.

When Mom got me the globe, she showed me where our city was on it. I'M HERE, I wrote, circling the spot.

Now I take my pen and scribble the same thing

on the corner of my desk, where the smooth desktop is chipped away down to the wood underneath.

I'M HERE, I write next to the names of other kids who sat here before. Then I add TO STAY.

I sign it with my initials to make it official: TF. Todd Foster.

7

"Look at that mess you left in the hall," Dad says when I get home. "There's mud and leaves all over the place."

After I clean that up I go and watch some cartoons.

"Turn that down! Some people are trying to read," Dad tells me.

So I turn down the volume. But then I get in trouble because I'm not using a coaster for my drink and I end up leaving water rings on the coffee table.

When Dad comes and sits on the couch beside me I stay real still and try not to do anything wrong. Only I just drank a can of Mountain Dew and all the fizz in my gut is trying to fight its way back up in a burp. I try to hold it back by swallowing a bunch of times but finally it comes out. Loud.

"*Uuurrp!*"

Dad looks over at me.

"Sorry," I say.

He's chewing on a big wad of gum—smoker's gum, the kind they give you when you're trying to quit. It has the ingredient that's in tobacco that gets you hooked on smoking. I tried a piece one time—tasted like the inside of an old shoe.

"I don't mean to be tough on you, Todd," he says. "It's just I feel like I'm going to jump out of my skin."

"Yeah. Well, you smell better now."

"I think I need more gum," he says.

"Can you fit any more in there?"

I'm not trying to joke but he starts laughing. So I start laughing, because I guess what I said was funny.

"If I run out of room I'll try squeezing it my ears and up my nose."

Seeing that picture in my head, I laugh harder. We watch some toons together.

Mom comes up from the basement, where she's been getting the laundry out of the dryer.

"Todd, don't you have a quiz tomorrow?" she asks.

Hearing that word *quiz* is like getting a snowball crammed down the back of my shirt.

"Yes."

"Is it a quiz on cartoons?" she says.

"Don't think so."

"Then you should hit the books before you hit the TV."

Mom's big on books. It's her job. She works three days a week down at the library, so she's always bringing home books for me and Christie.

"You heard the lady," Dad says. He reaches over and pulls one of his socks out of the laundry basket Mom's holding. Then he wraps it around my head like a blindfold and ties it in back. "Todd Foster, you have been condemned to go to your room and study." He lifts up the blindfold so I can see him. "Any last words?"

I can't think of any. But it doesn't matter, because the fizz from the Mountain Dew is still bubbling up in my gut and I can't hold back another—

"*Uuurrp!*"

Dad lowers the blindfold again. "Well said."

I feel my way over to the stairs and make my way up, peeking out from the bottom of the sock.

In my room it's just me and the books. We stare at each other. It's a standoff.

I don't really hate geography. I hate math and science, and they hate me back. But geography is kind of cool. I like maps and atlases. You can look at them and make like you're going on an adventure into the Amazon or Michigan. But when you have to remember names and dates, and who killed who, and what's a common denominator, I get lost.

But I can't tell Mr. Blaylock I'm lost. And if I ask too many questions he's going to know. So I keep quiet.

Last week we were learning all about birds, and I

was going to ask why the birds that go south for the winter come back in the summer. I mean, why not stay down south and just take it easy, like my grandparents down in Florida?

But I kept quiet, figuring it would be a dumb thing to say. Then Jackie the genius went and asked that same thing a minute later.

"Good question," Mr. B. told her.

That's *my* good question! I wanted to shout. I thought of it first!

"The answer is food," he said. "In the spring, all the insect eggs hatch in the north so there are plenty of bugs to fill the birds' bellies and feed their young."

I could have kicked myself for not speaking up. But I guess it's impossible to kick yourself unless you're double-jointed and you can kick your own butt.

Right now, I sit my butt down at my desk and lean back in the chair. Taped on the wall above the desk is a painting Eva did of me last year in Needs. We were supposed to do one of our desk partners. In the picture I've got big owl-sized brown eyes and ears big as wings. On top of my head are these silver streaks shooting out in all directions.

"Why do I have silver hair?" I asked her when she showed it to me.

"That's not hair. Those are sparks. Like in my birthday photo."

Eva was talking about a picture her mother took of us at her birthday party last year. Eva's crazy about sparklers, and we were goofing around with them when her mother snapped the shot. In the picture, I'm trying to write my name in the air with my sparkler, and Eva's holding hers behind my head, so it looks like my head is throwing off sparks.

"Are my ears really that big?" I asked when I saw her painting of me.

"Bigger!" She laughed.

"And my head's like one huge sparkler?"

Eva nodded. "But those aren't just any sparks. They're your smart sparks."

Eva thought I was some kind of genius, because back in Needs I knew all the answers.

Now I pull out my geography notes and open my atlas to the United States. There's a million rivers and lakes and state capitals I have to memorize. It's impossible. I mean, who ever heard of Boise, Idaho?

I scratch my head, waiting for the sparks to start flying.

8

At the start of last year, they brought in a head doctor to find out what was wrong with me. That's not how they said it. The teacher said the doctor just wanted to find out what I was good at and where I needed help.

Only, the test they gave me wasn't a real test. I didn't have to name state capitals or do long division. First they told me to draw a picture of me watching TV with my family. So I drew us all on the couch, with me on one end next to Mom and Christie way on the other end next to Dad. I drew Christie with fangs and big witch hair. I thought it was funny. Then the doctor looked at it and said, "Is this finished?"

And I got all worried that I'd left something out, but I couldn't figure what. This wasn't like a multiple choice where you get a chance even if you guess.

So I just shrugged and said, "Yeah. Maybe."

Then the doctor told me to remember four things.

"A blue barn. A hairy spider. Thomas Jefferson. And the number sixty-eight," she said. "Can you repeat those back to me?"

"A barn. Hairy spider. Thomas Jefferson. And number sixty . . . sixty . . ." I squeezed my eyes shut tight and tried to see the number, but it was all smudged in my brain.

"Sixty-eight," she told me.

"Right. Sixty-eight."

"Now let me tell you a story about how the monarch butterfly migrates from here all the way to Mexico every year."

First I thought the doctor had gone nuts. She was going all over the place and not making any sense, like she was a TV clicking through thirty channels a second so you can't really tell what you're looking at. What does Thomas Jefferson have to do with butterflies? But after a while I got into the butterfly story. They're so small and easy to break, but they fly thousands of miles just to go home for the winter, and then they come back.

It was a good story, and I was never going to look at a monarch butterfly the same way again. But then the story ended and the doctor asked me to tell her the four things I was supposed to remember.

If she wanted me to remember those things, why did she go blabbing about the butterflies?

"Ummm," I said. "Okay. President Lincoln? He

had some hair—some big hair? No. No. That's not right. President Lincoln lived in a barn, with his hair—and there were lots of spiders—when he was six?"

The doctor didn't nod or shake her head. She wrote something on her pad of paper, and I got really jumpy because I couldn't tell if I was doing good or really bad.

"Did I get any right?" I asked.

She gave me a nice smile, the same one she had when she was talking about butterflies. "Our meeting here today isn't about right and wrong. I want to get to know about you."

Two weeks later I was dumped in Special Needs.

First day in Needs. The kids looked normal, except for Harvey. He was sitting at his desk kissing the back of his hand for no reason.

"Everybody, this is Todd," Miss Wisswell told the class.

A couple of kids said, "Hi, Todd." I grunted and made a little wave back.

"Now we just have to find you a seat."

"He can sit here," said one of the girls. She had weird glasses on with pink lenses instead of clear, so I couldn't tell if she really needed them to see. "You sit here. You're my partner."

That was Eva. She's like that—bossy, but in a good way. She tells you to do stuff and if you don't she gets this confused look on her face, like you just turned her world upside down.

Eva took charge of me right from the start and showed me how things work in Special Needs.

"This is my desk. That's Harvey." She pointed him out as he was coming over to us. "You sit back down, Harvey. Nobody wants to be kissed by your stinky lips." He turned around and went back to his seat. "If he gets close he'll try and lay one on you. Don't let him. He kisses the gerbils and the lizard."

Eva pointed over to the counter behind the teacher's desk, where they had a big aquarium and two terrariums. Gerbils, lizards, and little flashy-blue fish were kept there.

"That's the zoo. No tapping the glass. No feeding unless Miss Wisswell is watching."

The fish aquarium was in the middle between the terrariums. One of the gerbils was clawing at the glass like he wanted to get in there with the fish and go for a swim.

"These are my other glasses," Eva said, showing me another pair with orange lenses. "I've got more at home. Green and purple. See over there? That's—"

"Why?" I broke in on her.

Eva looked all confused because I'd interrupted her speech.

"Why do you have those colored glasses?" I asked. "Doesn't it make things look all weird?"

She looked at me through her pink lenses. "It makes things look pretty. Even Harvey. Here, try on the orange ones."

I looked around first to make sure nobody was watching, but they were all doing pastel drawings of a bald eagle photo that was hanging on the blackboard. So I slipped the glasses on.

Everything looked freaky. The kids all had bright orange skin, like the guy who ate way too many carrots. It was like being underwater in orange juice. The sky outside the window looked like a wild sunset.

I took them off again and the world went back to plain colors.

"You wear these all the time?" I asked her.

Eva shook her head. "Just when I get bored of seeing the same things. It's like painting everything a different color every day."

That's what Eva's like. She sees more colors than everybody else.

I fall in the cracks, that's what Mom told me. I don't really belong in Special Needs because they don't move fast enough for me. And the regular class doesn't go slow enough. Mom promised it would only be for a while. But it felt like a life sentence.

The thing I never got about Needs was how they went slower than the normal class so we could catch up. I mean, if you have two cars and one is going a hundred miles an hour and the other is going two miles, the slow one is never going to catch up.

Mom told me some of what the head doctor said. My reading comprehension is poor. That means I don't understand what I'm reading most times. And they said I have weak memorization skills. But I could tell you the score in last year's Super Bowl. I bet the doctor wouldn't know that.

The only nice thing they said about me was I have a strong imagination. But what good is that? They never test you on making things up.

On the last day of fourth grade I got my report card.

"Good work, Todd," Miss Wisswell told me when she handed it over.

I stared at the outside of the card while everybody was tearing theirs open. It was like on TV when the jury comes back in with their verdict on a slip of paper.

"Look." Eva gave me a nudge, sitting in the next chair. "I got an Excellent in art."

She was wearing blue glasses that day, the ones that make you feel like you're living underwater. "Aren't you gonna open yours?"

I turned the card around in my hand, trying to see through the paper. Getting bad news is like ripping off a Band-Aid—better just to do it quick and get it over with. So I ripped it open.

Not guilty. Not guilty of being brain-dead. I did it. I made it back with the normal kids.

"What's it say?" Eva asked.

"Says I'm going back to the regular class. Fifth grade."

My smile was so wide I was showing every tooth in my head. Eva wasn't smiling back. Her eyes behind the blue lenses looked sad.

"Who's going to sit in your chair?" she said, all confused.

"I don't know. Somebody else?"

"But you're my partner."

"I'll still see you around," I told her. "We're going to see that movie next week, right?"

"But what about next year?"

I didn't have an answer for her.

When I got home there was a cake waiting for me. Mom made it with one of her cake molds, the one that's shaped like a turtle's shell.

"Why is it gray?" I asked, poking my finger in the icing.

"It's supposed to look like a brain, see? And brains are gray-colored." She started laughing. "Pretty funny, huh?"

"But why?"

Mom started slicing it up. "Because I knew you could do it."

"What if I failed?" I asked.

She handed me a plate. "You've still got brains. I've seen you in action. You've got the right stuff."

Christie came in the kitchen and said, "It's gray."

"It's really white-chocolate icing with a little food coloring," Mom told her. "It tastes great."

"Why is it shaped like that?"

"It's a brain," I said.

Christie made a face. "Well, I guess you could use one."

"Christie! Do *not* talk to your brother like that," Mom told her. "Be nice. This is a celebration for Todd."

I held up my report card. "I passed. I get to go back to the regular class next year, with the normal kids."

Christie whipped the card out of my hand and read it. I was expecting her to say something nasty and smart.

"Not bad," she told me. "Good for you. So, are we going to eat some brain cake or what?"

Getting a *not bad* from Christie was like winning an Oscar or the Super Bowl.

We all chowed down on the best gray brain-cake I ever tasted.

9

Okay. I'm in the zone. I'm going to ace this geography quiz.

"You've got fifteen minutes," Mr. Blaylock tells us, looking over at the clock on the wall. "On your mark. Get set. Go!"

Name the five Great Lakes is the first question.

I reach down in my brain and pull out Lake Michigan. That's one. Next. I close my eyes and look around inside my head. It's really dark in there and I don't see any more lakes.

There's got to be four more in there. I know I read about them last night. One had a name that made me think of Christie. I remember Mom telling her . . . to stop acting all superior. Right. Lake Superior. That makes two.

And there was one that had a name that didn't

make sense. Erie. Lake Erie. I remember thinking if you're going to call something Erie it should at least look something like an ear.

Two more left. Come on. I know the answers are in here somewhere. I squeezed them in last night.

I'll come back to that question.

State capitals is next.

North Dakota. South Dakota. Those are tough. Why do they have two Dakotas anyway? Why not just have one big one? Then I'd only have to know one capital. I leave those blank. I'll get back to them.

Oklahoma is easy: it's Oklahoma City. The Dakotas could learn a lesson from that.

For New York State it's a trick question, because you think it's got to be New York City. But it's really some place called Albany.

For Georgia it's Atlanta. Tennessee is Nashville.

Florida's capital must be Miami, because that's where the Miami Dolphins play. For Texas it should be Dallas, because of the Dallas Cowboys. It's a good thing Dad watches so much football.

Then there's a multiple choice on what state has what rivers and mountains. I like multiples—even if you guess you've got a shot.

At the bottom of the page they have the outlined shapes of different states, and you're supposed to fill in the name.

One looks sort of like a lumpy banana that somebody stepped on. It might be . . . Florida? Another state is shaped like a pot, with a handle and everything. I'll call it . . . Montana. I guess I've got a one-in-fifty chance. That's better than the lottery.

"And . . . time's up," Mr. B. says. "Pencils down."

What about all those questions I was going to get back to? All those blank spots on the page—they're like soldiers on a battlefield I promised I'd come back for. But I can't save them.

"Pass your sheets to the front."

When I get the sheets from the two kids behind me, I take a peek to see what they filled in.

Oh, no! The capital of Texas is some place called Austin. And the state shaped like a pot is Oklahoma.

At least I got the banana right. I should—I've eaten enough of them. Dad says they're good brain food, so I've gone on the Banana Diet. That's three bananas a day, even when I'm sick of them.

I'll eat anything to grow a brain.

10

I'm sitting on the grass by the front doors, waiting for Dad to pick me up after school.

"Hey, Todd," a voice says. Not "Hey, Gump" or "Hey, Mr. Retardo."

I look around and it's Harvey.

"Hi, Harvey."

He sits down beside me. I look around to make sure nobody's watching. Harvey's okay, but he always has these stains on his shirt, and his pants are way too short. He's lucky they can't assassinate you for being a slob.

"Hey, you remember my name!" he says, like it's a magic trick.

"Of course I remember your name."

Since I changed classes the kids from Needs don't try and talk to me much anymore. They think

I'm like some kind of genius now. The first day back in school Harvey saw me going into Mr. Blaylock's class.

"Where you going?" he asked.

I told him I wasn't in Needs anymore.

"Wow," he said, looking past me into the fifth-grade class. "Scary."

I just kind of shrugged. Scary was right. For a second there, standing in the doorway, I *really* wanted to follow him down the hall back to Needs, where nothing was ever scary.

Now he reaches into his jacket pocket. "I got something for you," he says. He hands me a crumpled paper bag. "It's from Eva. She said to say . . . She said, 'Give this to Todd so he won't yell at me.' Yeah, that's what she said."

Harvey stands up now.

"Hey, there's my dad," he shouts, surprised like he just spotted Bigfoot or something, like his dad doesn't pick him up every day at the same time. "I gotta go." He runs across the grass to a waiting car.

I open the paper bag. Inside I find two seashells, some sand, and a note printed in ten different colors of pencil crayon.

It says:

DEAR TOD, I MISS YOU

Under the words are about a hundred X's and O's. You know, like hugs and kisses. I think X's are supposed to mean kisses, and O's are hugs. I don't know why.

I turn the paper over, but that's all there is.

I rub the sand between my fingers over the open bag, careful not to lose any.

Mom usually picks me up after school, but she doesn't get off work today for another hour so Dad comes for me. I like riding with Mom better because she lets me choose the radio station. Dad listens to the all-news station—the all-boring one.

We drive over to the library to pick Mom up. She works there three days a week, finding books for people and answering questions.

"So what did you learn today?" Dad asks. "Anything good?"

"Found out that monkeys use tools," I say.

"Oh, yeah? Maybe we can get one over to fix the garage door."

I laugh. "Not those kinds of tools. They take twigs and stick them in termite nests to pull bugs out and eat them. And they use rocks to crack open nuts."

"Bugs and nuts? Stop, you're making me hungry."

Dad pulls over to the curb in front of the library. "We're fifteen minutes early," he says, turning up the radio to hear the local news.

"Can I go in and see Mom?"

"If you go now you'll miss the traffic report."

"Oh." I sag back in my seat.

"I'm kidding, kiddo," he tells me. "Sure. Go see your mom."

I jump out of the car and go inside. It's only a small library so it's not hard to find her.

Mom's in the kids' section, where there's a big mess of cushions tossed around on the floor and books spilling off the shelves. A bunch of mothers are here with little preschool kids. The library has story times in the afternoon—songs and puppets, that kind of stuff. When she's not answering questions, Mom does the afternoon story.

"Can I try? Can I try?" a girl squeals.

Mom's holding her guitar out so the kid can pluck the strings. *Twing-twang.* The girl squeals some more.

"Not bad," Mom tells her.

The crowd is breaking up and Mom starts packing her things away. She sets the guitar down in its old beaten-up case and clicks the latches shut.

There was this one song she used to sing to me, even before I was born. Mom said she'd rest the guitar on her belly right on top of me and play my favorite song, the one she said always made me kick. It's an old one from when she was a kid, called "Wild Thing." She says it's my song because that's what I was like before I was born.

"You were like a tiny little kung fu master," she told me. "Kicking and chopping and somersaulting all over the place in there."

51

Mom spots me now. "Todd. Come help me tidy up."

I put some books back on the shelf for her and gather up a bunch of finger puppets from the floor. They're all barnyard animals with googly eyes.

By the time I've got the cushions stacked up, the other librarian has kicked everybody out and they start turning off the lights.

"Let's hurry before we get locked in," Mom says, going to get her coat.

Being locked in the library overnight would be on my list of top ten nightmares. Trapped with all these books too hard for me to read—all those pages crammed with stuff I'm supposed to know. For me, that's worse than killer sharks or bloodthirsty ghosts.

Mom and the other librarian close up and I help carry Mom's bag filled with books out to the car.

"How's my rock star?" Dad asks Mom when she stuffs the guitar in the backseat beside me.

"Hungry," she says.

"Really. Todd was just telling me how to eat termites."

"I'm not *that* hungry," Mom says. She starts searching through the stations on the radio.

"Hey, I was listening to the news."

Mom keeps searching. "No. We need something lively, something to get our hearts pumping. Right, Todd?" She peeks back at me over the headrest.

"Right."

Mom finds some funky dance music and turns up

the volume. Dad grunts and shakes his head, pulling away from the curb for home. Mom drums her fingers on the dashboard, and by the time we stop at the first light even Dad's tapping his thumbs on the steering wheel, keeping the beat.

Me, I'm doing a drum solo on Mom's guitar case. It used to bug me that she did songs for other kids. I mean, she's only supposed to do that kind of stuff for me, and maybe Christie. She's *our* mom. But then she told me she never ever sings my song for anybody else.

"You're my only wild thing," she said.

So then it was okay.

11

"Okay, I gotta run," Dad says, stuffing half a bacon sandwich in his mouth and grabbing his jacket from the back of his chair. He gives Mom a bacon kiss on the cheek.

"Todd," he says, swallowing, "you've got your assignment?" He says "assignment" like I'm a spy going undercover or something.

I nod. I'm supposed to rake the leaves off the front lawn. And get paid four dollars.

It's Saturday but he's working overtime down at the factory, where he drives a forklift that can pick up three tons of stuff.

When Dad's gone, Mom goes back to making breakfast. Some kind of eggs. On Saturday morning Mom always makes me eat breakfast before I can watch any cartoons. It's the law.

"You still look sleepy," she tells me. Her hair is messed up from bed. I like how she looks in the morning, before she puts her makeup on. Only *we* get to see her real face. Everybody outside sees her made-up one.

"I had nightmares last night," I say.

"What kind of nightmares?"

Mom flips the eggs half over on top of shredded cheese in the middle. Must be an omelet.

"They were these crazy dreams where the bus gets lost taking me to school and my whole class ends up on a deserted island. There's nothing to eat there except bugs and bananas. So the kids all get together and decide they're going to eat me for lunch. I start running, but they're faster than me and they chase me right off the edge of a cliff. But I wake up before I hit the ground."

"That's a nasty dream," Mom says.

I hear a snort from behind me. Christie says, "Next time you go to bed, pack a parachute."

I try to think of something to say. Just once I want to have something to say back. But I take too long and she starts talking again.

"What's cooking?"

Mom hands her a glass of orange juice. "Go sit on the couch and I'll bring you your eggs in a minute."

Christie goes to the living room and I can hear her turning the TV on.

"Mom, she's got the TV on. Before breakfast," I tell her.

"Oh, let her watch. Stay with me for a while."

Mom starts chopping up bananas for her smoothie. She puts some milk in the blender and adds this green powder that's made up of vegetables and seaweed and some kind of grass you can eat. I call it Pond Juice, because it looks like you just dipped your glass in a frog pond and came up with a pile of green slimy stuff.

"Can you make some for me too?" I ask.

"You hate my green juice," Mom says.

"Yeah. But Dad said it's brain food."

Mom adds some extra powder and fruit. "Well, that's true."

She fires up the blender and then pours a glass for her and one for me. Holding my breath, and my nose, I try and down it as fast as I can. I get almost to the bottom. Pond Juice squirts up the back of my nose. I put the glass on the counter and Mom hands me paper towels.

"Good, huh?" she says, smiling and shaking her head.

I use the towels to blow the frog soup out of my nose.

"Tastes like dirt and bananas," I say.

Using the spatula, Mom cuts the omelet in two and hands me a plate. "This will kill the taste."

She takes the other half out to Christie.

I use a leftover paper towel to wipe off my tongue.

"Honey, don't let your sister get to you," Mom tells me, coming back and taking a gulp of her juice.

"She always knows the exact worst thing to say." I start in on my eggs.

"She does have a bit of a mean streak, and a smart mouth. But don't worry, we'll work on her. Train her to be nicer."

"Good luck," I say.

Mom smiles at me. When other people smile at me, I kind of have to figure out why they're smiling. Like maybe they're making fun of me, laughing at me, or just waiting for me to give the wrong answer. But with Mom, her smile only means one thing—she loves me.

"Tell me more about your dream," she says. "Sometimes if you talk about your nightmares they go away."

I tell her what the deserted island was like. And how real it felt falling off that cliff, with the wind in my face and that roller-coaster feeling in my gut.

"Pretty scary," Mom says.

"Yeah. It felt like school."

12

Raking is a lot of work. I wish I had one of those leaf blowers like the guy across the street. He doesn't have to drag a heavy rake around. All he does is point and blow. I wonder if I could use Christie's hair dryer to do that.

But we probably don't have an extension cord long enough.

I pick a corner of the lawn and start raking. Our house has two trees. One in the front yard and one in back. But leaves blow over from our neighbors' too, so there's like a whole forest of leaves here, enough to fill a garbage bag just out front.

Last fall we did a leaf project in Needs and Eva came over to hunt for good ones.

We needed eight kinds of leaves. Miss Wisswell was going to show us how to make a little book of pressed leaves out of them. If you press them the right way, they stay the same color and don't get old, like mummies, Miss W. said. Leaf mummies.

"What's this one's name?" Eva asked me when we were searching around on the lawn.

She'd hold up a leaf and I'd look in the guidebook to see what kind of tree it came from.

But she kept asking me about a new leaf every two seconds, so I just started making up names for them.

"What's this one?" she said.

"Oh, that's Larry."

"How about this one?"

"That's King Kong."

"You're crazy," she told me, laughing. "You're King Crazy."

Then Eva took the Kong leaf and put it on top of my head like a crown.

She ended up taking about fifty leaves because she couldn't decide which ones looked best. Each one had a different pattern of colors, and she's nuts about colors.

When I'm done raking the front yard now I've got a pile that's chest-high on me. I drag the rake out back and keep going.

Under the oak tree in back there's no marker or anything, no little gravestone, but I know exactly where Psycho's buried. I've been leaving sunflower seeds there for him. I know the birds and squirrels just take them, but I like doing it anyway.

I keep finding his stuff hiding around my room. Last night I found one of his old chewed-up toilet paper rolls. It got me thinking about that time me and Eva built him an obstacle course. We had paper towel rolls set up like tunnels he'd run through, some hurdles we made out of Fudgesicle sticks glued together, and a cardboard ramp he had to climb.

We were training him for the mouse Olympics. But he had other ideas. I've heard of mice that find their way through complicated mazes to get cheese and stuff, but Psycho wasn't that kind of mouse.

Eva was keeping time on her watch to see how fast he went. When she said go I set him loose.

He went into the first tunnel on the course all right, but he wouldn't come out of it. After about twenty seconds I got down and put my head to the floor to check on him. There he was, in the middle of the obstacle course, taking a nap.

"Hey, wake up," I told him. "This is supposed to be a race."

But he just lay there, eyes shut, dreaming mouse dreams.

"Here," Eva said. "Try a sunflower seed."

I held the seed at the end of the tunnel and waved it around so he could smell it, but he wouldn't budge.

"Wake up! Wake up!" Eva called to him.

"What's going on?" Christie said, standing by the door to my room. "What's with all the noise?"

"Psycho's running the obstacle course, only he's

not running anymore. He fell asleep inside the roll, and he won't come out. We're losing time." Eva said all that in one breath. When she gets excited she'll keep going until she runs out of air. "Hold it. I know. Peanut butter. That's his favorite. Do you have peanut butter?"

Christie nodded. "Yeah, down in the fridge."

"Quick, we have to get some." Eva got up and grabbed my sister's hand, pulling her out the door. "I think he likes the crunchy kind best."

Before she disappeared into the hall, Christie shot me a look that said, "Where's this crazy person taking me?"

Any other day at my house Christie would be in charge, but when Eva gets all worked up nothing can stop her.

They got back in record time with a jar of crunchy peanut butter. Christie opened it and Eva scooped some out with her finger. She crouched down and stuck it in the end of the tunnel.

We were all quiet a second, waiting to see if it would work. Then Eva made a little squeak. "He just nibbled my finger."

Psycho poked his head out and looked around.

"The hurdles are next," I said. "Jump the hurdles."

He sniffed the air like he was searching for more peanut butter. Eva showed him the finger he'd nibbled on and led him to the first hurdle. Mice don't really jump too much, unless you scare them, and then they only jump straight up in the air. So Psycho just sort of walked over the hurdle, knocking it down.

It took three more finger scoops from the peanut butter jar to get him through the last tunnel and over the finish line.

"Time?" I asked.

Eva checked. "He ran it in five minutes and forty-five seconds. But that's counting his three-minute nap in the tunnel." She turned to Christie. "Is that good?"

"How many mice have run this course before?"

"He's the first," Eva says.

"Well, then he set a record, didn't he?" Christie said to her, crouching down to give Psycho a little pat between the ears with her pinky.

I poured Psycho a pile of sunflower seeds, since we didn't have a gold medal for him.

When I'm done piling leaves in the backyard, I go get a garbage bag. Before I start stuffing them in, I pick one off the pile. It's all bright yellow and orange. If Eva was here I'd give it to her. It's too perfect to put in the garbage.

I carry it over to Psycho's spot under the oak tree. When the sun hits that leaf just right it looks a little like gold.

13

Back when I was in grade two and I believed everything Christie said, she told me that chalk was made from dead people's bones. She said they took skeletons and smashed them into powder, then melted the powder to pour into chalk molds. So every time the teacher would write on the blackboard I'd get the shivers.

Now I know better, but I still get that feeling like a spider's running up my back when Mr. Blaylock picks up the chalk and starts writing.

"It's time to talk about the subject of your history project," Mr. B. says. "It will be due in exactly ten days. It has to be at least two pages long. That's two written pages. If you want you can include a piece of art with that too. A drawing, a painting, whatever you like."

He moves away from the board so we can see what he wrote.

OTA BENGA.

He underlines it twice.

"Jackie, can you hand out these worksheets?"

He gives her a stack of pages, and she walks up and down the rows handing them out.

"Ota Benga," Mr. Blaylock says, "was the name of a man from Africa who was displayed in the monkey house of the Bronx Zoo in 1906. He was what they used to call a Pygmy, which is a race of short, black-skinned people in Africa. Now, how many of you have been to a zoo?"

Everybody holds up their hands.

"What do they have at the zoo?"

Lions, someone says. Penguins, says a boy up front. Bears, says someone else. Parrots. Elephants. Alligators. I keep quiet. I want to say chimpanzees. But what if I'm wrong?

"So, what do all these things have in common?" Mr. Blaylock asks. "Jackie?" He calls on her because her hand is always up first. In a few years she'll have an arm big as the Incredible Hulk's from raising her hand so much.

"They're all animals," she says.

"Exactly. So, why would they keep this man, Ota Benga, in a zoo?"

I never raise my hand anymore. What's the use? But I'm thinking that maybe this man committed a crime, maybe he stole a car, so they put him in the zoo.

"Maybe if he killed somebody?" Zero says.

Mr. Blaylock shakes his head at him. It feels good not to get that head shake aimed at me.

"No. If you kill someone you go to jail. Not to the zoo."

Mr. Blaylock waits a minute for another answer. No one makes a sound. Mr. B. looks around at the class. I look at the floor.

"The only reason they would keep a man in a zoo was if they thought he was just another animal, like a hippo or a gorilla."

He reaches up and pulls down the projector screen that hangs above the blackboard.

"Now, I'm going to show you some slides so you can see what Ota Benga looked like. Ronald, shut the blinds, please."

Mr. Blaylock flicks the light switch and walks to the back of the dark room. A bright white square flashes on the screen. There's a click from the slide projector.

The white square is replaced by a picture of a black man holding a chimpanzee. He's dressed like Tarzan, no shirt or anything, just some cloth tied around his waist instead of pants. He looks sad, and the chimp seems sad too.

"This photo was taken in the park at the Bronx Zoo. That's Ota Benga with a chimpanzee named

Polly who was from the Congo, just like Ota. The Congo is a country right in the middle of Africa."

The projector clicks again.

"In this picture Ota is showing off his pointed teeth. Many different peoples around the world file their teeth into sharp points like that. It isn't done to help with eating or fighting, they just like the way it looks. Here in America we get braces to straighten our teeth. The Pygmies sharpen theirs. Looks scary, doesn't it?"

I nod to myself. Those teeth look sharp enough to cut glass.

"They charged a dime to take a photo of Ota Benga showing his teeth. Sometimes the keepers at the zoo would tell him to rush the bars of his cage and bare his teeth to the crowds watching."

There is another click and a new picture flashes on the screen.

"Here he is with some of his Pygmy friends at the St. Louis World's Fair at the beginning of the century. An American explorer brought the Pygmies over from Africa to display them at the fair. The Pygmies were called savages and treated like animals to entertain the crowds."

On the screen they were all standing close together, waiting for the picture-taking to be over, I guess.

Mr. Blaylock turns the projector off and puts the lights back on.

"We'll talk more about Ota Benga during our

history hour over the next few days. There are all kinds of books on the Congo and Africa in the library. And you can use the CD-ROM library on the computer to research Africa, its peoples, the land and animals. The pictures I showed you are printed on your worksheets."

He pulls the screen back up so we can see the blackboard again.

OTA BENGA.

"He is the subject of your project. Ota was taken from the wilds of Africa to New York City. During the day they made him perform in his cage, and at night he slept in a hammock in the monkey house. You can write about life in the Congo and Ota's people. Or you can write about New York at the turn of the century and the Bronx Zoo. Whatever you like. But I want you to tie it in to Ota. Tell me what you think his life was like."

Mr. Blaylock opens the blinds to let the afternoon sun in. "There's no right or wrong this time. Just give me your ideas. Remember, it has to be two pages long—and that doesn't mean you can just write really big, Ronald."

Everybody laughs, but not at me for once.

I flip through to the pictures in our worksheets. I like the photo of Ota hugging the chimp named Polly. They look sad, and they're a long way from home, but at least they're together.

14

After school me and Dad go to the barber to get scalped. My hair was just starting to grow back and look normal, but Dad says I'm getting kind of shaggy. I keep wanting to tell him it's not like I'm a soldier or something. But I guess I am in *Dad's* army, where there's only the two of us.

Even my mouse, Psycho, had longer hair than what I'm left with after a buzz cut. I don't want to go around balder than a mouse. But I don't want to let Dad down either. He likes us looking the same.

When we get to the barber a couple of guys are already sitting in chairs waiting their turn. There are mirrors everywhere so you can see your head from every angle. And you can see the big TV even if your chair is pointing the wrong way. Right now a football game is starting up. It's the Bills against the Dolphins.

"It'll be about a fifteen-minute wait," Larry the barber tells us.

"No problem," Dad says. "I'm just going to go grab something. Keep an eye on my kid, okay, Larry?"

"Sure."

Dad tells me to watch the game and he'll be back in a minute. "Who do we like to win?" he asks.

"Dolphins," I say. Dad's been a big Miami fan since he was a kid.

He leaves and I watch the Bills fumble the kickoff, losing the ball on the first play.

"Look at that," Larry says. "He gets paid a million dollars to lose the ball. I can lose it for free."

The other guys grunt about the crazy money players make. I nod with them.

The man next to me goes up for his cut, leaving me next. The Dolphins run a quarterback sneak and score a touchdown. I can't believe Dad's missing this.

"I'm going to go get my dad," I tell Larry.

"Sure, kid."

Dad's going to be happy the Fish are winning. I walk up a few stores, looking through the windows for him. Then I look over toward the parking lot. There he is, leaning on the hood of our car.

And he's smoking! Dad's smoking!

Mom's really not going to like that. She keeps telling him he's going to have a heart attack if he doesn't quit. And he promised her he was. I even heard him say it, with his hand over his heart.

He sees me seeing him and pushes off from the hood, flicking the cigarette away into the parking lot.

"Is it our turn?" he asks, walking over to me.

I nod. "Almost."

He pulls a stick of gum out of his pocket, real gum, not the smoker's kind. "Gum?"

I take a piece too. He always used to chew spearmint gum after smoking, to kill the smell on his breath. We stand there chewing a minute, watching the people go by.

"It's tough," Dad says finally.

First I think he's talking about the gum, like maybe it's really old or something. But then I get it.

"I know it's not good to keep secrets," Dad says. "But do you think we can keep this one from your mother? I mean, I really am quitting. It's just some days my brain is screaming for a cigarette."

I nod, even though I don't get it.

"I won't tell," I say. I kind of like having a secret with Dad.

"I don't want to disappoint your mother," Dad tells me.

"Yeah. Maybe I can tell you a secret too? Like a top secret?"

"Go ahead."

I've been itching to tell someone almost as much

as Dad's been itching for a cigarette. "I'm not doing too hot in fifth grade. It's really hard, and I'm really trying. I got a C minus on my geography quiz. But I don't know if I'm going to make it."

Dad nods. "You know your teacher, Mr. . . . ?"

"Mr. Blaylock."

"Yeah. At the last parent-teacher meeting, he said he has a half-hour miniclass after school gets out, if you need extra help with anything."

That's just what I need, *more* school. "I know. But Jackie Williams goes to that class, and she's like a hundred times smarter than me. She doesn't even need it. Her brain's so full it's going to explode."

Dad laughs. "Still, let's give it a shot. At least you'll get more attention from the teacher, right? He seems like an okay guy."

"I guess."

We start to walk back to the barbershop.

"Don't tell Mom yet, okay?" I ask. "Mr. B. says if I improve in the next month I could still get a passing grade. I don't want to let Mom down."

Dad spits his gum in the garbage, so I spit mine out too.

"You won't be letting her down," he tells me. "You're trying hard. But I know what you mean. I don't want to let her down either."

Before we go back in the shop I stop and say, "Can I tell you one more secret?" I take a deep breath and blurt it out. "I don't want to get another buzz cut."

"Why not? It's the perfect cut. And besides, you'll look cool. Nobody will mess with you."

How can I explain it to him? Sometimes it's like he's living on another planet.

"Maybe when *you* were a kid it was cool. But now when I get buzzed they call me Gump at school, because of that movie where the guy had a freaky haircut. I only want to look like everybody else."

Dad's smiling at me, I don't know why.

"I said the same thing to my dad. A million years ago. Except he had a ponytail, and he wanted me to have one too." Dad shrugs. "Okay. But from now on I'm calling you Shaggy."

That's probably the best name I've ever been called, maybe even better that Todd.

Maybe because it's a name only Dad will call me.

15

Our class goes to the library to research our Ota Benga project. Jackie and some other kids are using the computers, looking up stuff on CD-ROMs.

We're here in the library for independent study.

"That means no talking and no passing notes," Mr. B. tells us. Like jail.

I sit staring at the cover of a book on elephants.

The library always makes me nervous—being surrounded by thousands of books. There's just too many of them to read. I'll never catch up.

My back is to the windows. I can feel the sun coming in. I close my eyes and imagine I'm outside, sitting on a bench watching elephants pass by. Then I hear Eva's voice coming from far away.

"What's this one?" she asks, calling out to someone.

I turn in my chair to look out the window. It's open a little and I can hear people moving around outside. The library is on the second floor, so I'm looking down at a bunch of kids in the field beside the school.

"That's another quartz," Miss Wisswell answers. I'd know her voice anywhere.

Down in the playground, the Needs class is kicking up rocks and looking in the dirt.

"Put that one in your bucket," Miss Wisswell says. "We're going to sort them all out back in class."

Rock collecting. I remember Miss W. saying we were going to do that in the class this year. Me and Eva have rock collections already. I've got mine set in my room on the window ledge. Eva keeps hers in a shoe box so they won't get dusty.

I see Harvey run up to Miss Wisswell, holding out his hand.

"Gold! I found gold!"

"Let's see," Miss W. says. She holds it in the sunlight. The other kids crowd around. "It looks like gold, doesn't it?" she asks, showing it to everybody. "But it's really called fool's gold. It's not worth anything, but it is pretty, isn't it, Harvey?"

"Can I keep it?" he says.

"Of course. Its scientific name is iron pyrites. The way I remember the name is to think 'iron pirates.' You know, like pirates who sail the seas in big ships and bury their treasure on deserted islands?"

"We did treasure maps last year," Eva says.

Miss Wisswell nods at her. "That's right. So, if you

were an iron pirate you would take your fool's gold and bury it. Where would you bury your treasure, Harvey?" She hands him the rock and he looks at her like she just did a magic trick or something.

"In my closet," he says. Eva and everybody laughs. Then Harvey joins in too.

What he said sounds like something I would say. It feels weird that I'm in here with all these books, with all the people who hate me, and they're all out-side laughing. I should be the one making Eva laugh.

We found stuff out together. Like rocks always look best when they're wet. And you can get shocks from licking a battery. And frogs get scared and go to the bathroom if you hold them too long.

Now all I'm finding out is what an idiot I am. And I already knew that. Back in Needs I was one of the smartest—other kids would even ask *me* for help.

I'd help out Eva. And she'd help me out sometimes too. She's not dumb. She just gets stuck on things, like when she's doing a test and doesn't know an answer, she won't skip it or come back to it later. She'll keep reading it over and over until the time runs out.

I wish Eva would look up right now, and then I would wave and she would wave and everything would be all right. But she's busy kicking up pirate rocks.

75

16

I wonder if long division ever killed anybody. I mean, like made their brains explode. I'm trying to divide 1,045 by 11. Every time I work out an answer it comes out different from the answer at the back of the textbook. See, the book gives you the answer, but Mr. Blaylock wants to see how you worked it out on paper. So you can't just cheat and use a calculator or copy from the book.

I've got my stuff spread out on the kitchen table. The kitchen's better for homework, because up in my room there's too much stuff to look at and I'll end up playing with my Game Boy or looking at comics.

But the bad thing about doing homework here is everybody's always coming in and getting stuff from the fridge and peeking over your shoulder to see what you're doing.

Like now, when I've got the eraser end of my

pencil pushing my nose up into a pig's snout, Christie walks in. She just got home from the mall, shopping with Mom. She puts her bags filled with clothes and junk on the other end of the table.

"Hey, hog-boy," she says.

I get rid of my snout.

She's got that sparkly makeup stuff on her eyelids. It's the only makeup Mom lets her wear out of the house. Eva went nuts the first time she saw Christie with it on. "What's that on your eyes?" she asked.

"It's called glitter."

Eva wanted to try some. So Christie handed her a little bottle of the junk.

"I need a mirror," Eva said, heading for the bathroom.

And when she came back she had glitter around her eyes, on her cheeks, her nose and forehead. She looked like some kind of alien kid.

Christie started laughing, but not a mean laugh. "I think you used a *little* too much. You look like you're sweating diamonds."

Then Eva started giggling with her. Christie helped her wipe some off with a hand towel. But even the next day in Needs, she still looked kind of sparkly.

Christie comes over now and spins my math book to see what I'm working on. "Long division," she says. "Wait till you get to geometry."

She grabs a Diet Coke from the fridge.

"I don't know," I say. "When the numbers get this big it's way harder."

She comes around the table, and I keep an eye on her in case she's going to punch me in the arm or flick my ears. But she's only trying to see what I've been writing in my workbook.

"Doesn't matter how big the numbers are," Christie tells me. "The rules don't change." She leans over to see my calculations. "Your remainder goes here, not on top."

She grabs my pencil and crosses out everything I've done. Then she writes in the problem again: $11\overline{)1045}$.

"You start by seeing if . . ." Christie leads me through the division. She always goes too fast, so I have to concentrate real hard.

When we were little it wasn't bad having a big sister. I'd ask her a million questions and follow her around because she knew how stuff worked. But when I was the last to learn how to tie my shoes, Christie wouldn't let me go anywhere with her in my Velcro sneakers.

"See," she says now, handing me the pencil. "Now you do one."

The next problem has even bigger numbers. I start in on it, putting my remainder in the right place this time. "Thanks for helping me."

"Yeah, bro," she says, taking a sip of her Coke. "You can thank me by getting this one right."

I like it when she calls me bro. *Todd* doesn't really mean anything, but *bro* means I'm her *brother*.

17

"Hey, Gump!" Zero says, leaning across the back of my seat on the school bus. He says the *p* in *Gump* so hard I can feel him spitting on my neck.

Mr. B. turns away from talking to the driver.

"Ronald! Glue your backside to that seat," he says.

Zero glues himself but kicks the back of my seat until the bus starts up and Mr. B. comes over to sit beside me. We're right behind where the front doors open.

"So, have you been to the science center before?" he asks.

"No. But we went to the zoo last year."

Mr. B. must be about twice as big as Dad. I wonder what he ate when he was a kid. And where can I get some of that muscle food? But maybe he was just born big, like Christie was born mean.

"Well, they have a miniature zoo at the science center for insects. You can look at all kinds of bugs and spiders. Even scorpions."

I'm thinking, Why does he even talk to me? I mean, why not Jackie, she's the smartest?

"Tarantulas?" I ask him.

"Oh, yeah." He waves his fingers in the air like they're spider legs. "Have you ever touched one?"

I shake my head. "They're poison."

"In the wild they are. But when they're kept as pets they get the poison taken out of them. In the terrarium I had growing up, I kept a big hairy tarantula."

"You ever touch it?" I ask.

"Yeah. You can pet them once they get used to you."

Behind us in the bus everybody's talking.

"Time to check Gump's diaper," someone yells out.

"Keep it down back there," Mr. B. calls out.

I've been hearing that joke for weeks now. Check Gump's diaper. Ever since we were doing drawing in class and I kind of had my thumb in my mouth. Not like I was sucking it like a baby. I was just sort of chewing on it. Concentrating. Now they won't shut up about it.

I look over and see Mr. Blaylock looking sideways at me.

"You know, when I was ten years old I used to get beat up a lot," he says to me.

"By who?"

"The other kids."

"But you're big," I tell him, like he doesn't know it already.

He nods. "I was big then, too. Bigger than the other kids. But it was as if the names they called me cut me down. Made me small."

I can't picture anybody hitting Mr. Blaylock. Even if he was shrunk to ten years old, I'm sure he could squash me like a bug.

"Is that a true story?" I ask him. Sometimes I hear a story I think is real, but it ends up being just made up. Christie does that to me all the time.

"True story," he says, smiling down at me.

They pushed him around like they push me around. They called him names just like they call me. Maybe different names, but still.

The names didn't kill him.

18

I'm eating a banana when the phone rings. I really hate bananas, ever since I peeled one without looking and took a big bite of a rotten, mushy brown one. I had to go brush my tongue with toothpaste to get rid of the taste. But bananas are brain food.

I'm trying hard not to think about what I'm eating when I reach over and pick up the phone.

Before I say hello, I remember I'm not supposed to answer the phone, because what if it's Eva? What am I going to say?

So I stop chewing and just listen, trying to tell who's on the other end by the way they're breathing.

"Somebody there?" a voice asks. Eva's voice.

I try and think if I can hang up without her knowing I'm here. But then she says—

"Todd? You there?"

"Yeah. I'm here."

"You're supposed to say hello when you pick up the phone."

"Hello."

"Where you been?" Eva says. "I've been trying to call you for a week."

"Well, I have to rake the leaves off the lawn all the time. It's my job. Keeps me really busy." After I say that I hear how dumb it sounds.

"I called to tell you October fifteenth is next Tuesday."

"What's October fifteenth?"

"It's my birthday. I'm having a party at my place. All the kids from class are coming. We're going to have two and a half kinds of cake. The half part is for Tracy, remember she's allergic to everything, so it'll be a cake with nothing in it. And there's going to be movies and karaoke and sparklers and . . ."

Eva has to stop now and I can hear her panting on the other end.

I can just see it in my head, a party with all the Needs kids running around and Harvey kissing everybody in sight.

"I don't know, Eva. I have to do something on Tuesday."

She's quiet for a second. "What do you mean?" she asks.

"I've got this big project, and a lot of homework.

And stuff, lots of stuff." I'm real bad at lying to most people, but I'm even worse at lying to Eva.

"You have to come," she tells me. "I invited you. You can't say no."

That's *so* Eva.

"But we're partners," she goes on when I don't say anything. "Who am I gonna sing karaoke with?"

"I don't know," I say. "Listen, I gotta go. Someone's knocking on my door."

"But—" she starts.

"Gotta go," I say.

"But—"

"Sorry," I tell her. "Bye."

I'm sweating when I hang up. I can see her on the other end, sitting in her living room, still saying "but" into the phone.

19

I pull my inflatable globe out of my closet. It dribbles pretty good on the hardwood floor in my room. There's the Congo on the bottom half of the globe, right in the middle of Africa.

That's where Ota Benga was from.

I have to write two pages and maybe do a piece of art. How am I supposed to write two whole pages?

"There are books in the library with a thousand pages in them," Miss Wisswell used to say to us. "And someone wrote all those words, one at a time. Just like you write one word at a time."

She made it sound easy.

I take out the worksheets Mr. Blaylock gave us. The pictures from the slide show are printed on the last couple of pages. I tape them up on the wall behind my desk.

I stare at page one of the handouts and start reading, one word at a time.

Ota Benga. They put him in the monkey house with chimps and orangutans. They thought he was just another animal. But why? I mean, he looks normal. You can't really tell from the pictures that he's so short. He wasn't even short like a dwarf or a Munchkin. And even if he was Munchkin-sized, they can't lock you up for that. He was a grown man, the worksheet says, in his early twenties.

I bounce my globe on the floor.

Gotta do good on this! Gotta act smart, I tell myself.

I'm failing so bad I need to get a B or a B- on this project. I have to. Gotta squeeze some juice out of my brain. I stop and look at Eva's picture of me with the sparks coming out of my head.

"Congo. Congo." I say it to the beat of the bouncing globe, trying to wake up some smart sparks.

"Con-go. Con-go."

Nothing's coming into my head. Sometimes I say a word over and over so many times, even a regular word like *apple,* that I start to forget what it means.

I go back to my desk and read more about Ota Benga.

Sometimes they let him out to walk around the zoo. They made him wear a white suit. It was like a disguise so he could walk around like everybody else looking at the animals. When he wore it, people would treat him like a real person, not an animal.

He hung around the seal pool during feeding time, when the keepers tossed fish into the air from big buckets for the seals to catch. Ota visited the lion house and the elephant house. Back in Africa, he used to hunt the huge elephants with bows and arrows. At the Bronx Zoo they let you come right up close and pat them, and the elephants wouldn't stomp on him like they would back home.

But the keepers wouldn't let him stay in the real world for too long. He had to take off his suit and go back in his cage so the crowds could look at him.

Ota Benga was the most popular exhibit at the zoo.

The New York Times newspaper wrote:

Nearly every man, woman, and child of this crowd made for the monkey house to see the star attraction in the park—the wild man from Africa. They chased him about the grounds all day, howling, jeering and yelling. Some of them poked him in the ribs, others tripped him up, all laughed at him.

The zookeepers used to throw bones on the floor of his cage to make him look like a savage.

The crowds laughed at everything he did, even when he just stood there drinking sodas, like he was a dog doing a trick.

All this stuff is so hard to read. I don't mean it has big words or anything, just that it's so sad.

I look above my desk at the picture of Ota Benga holding Polly the chimp. The more I read about him, the sadder he looks standing there.

Maybe the only happy thing that happened to him at the zoo was that he got to make friends with Polly and Dohong. He knew Polly from before he came to the zoo and tried to take care of her and help her get used to the strange new place. Dohong was an orangutan. Harvey would love Dohong, because Harvey always wanted to be a monkey, running around hooting and grunting like one. Orangutans come from Asia, so Ota had never seen one before. They have orange tufty hair and have really long arms for swinging in the trees.

Dohong was the smartest monkey Ota had ever met. There was a trapeze, like they have in circuses, set up in his cage for him to play on. It says in the worksheets that sometimes Dohong would wedge the wooden swing part of the trapeze between the bars to make the space between the bars wider.

Ota saw that Dohong was planning an escape and helped him, trying to make the space big enough to squeeze Dohong through.

Even after Ota Benga left the zoo forever, Dohong was still there, getting the chimps to help him crack and bend the bars of his cage. He never did escape, though.

So now I know all this stuff about Ota Benga. I get a pencil and sharpen it a few times. One word at a time, I tell myself. Don't think two pages, just think one word.

But what word? What am I supposed to write? They tell you to write a project, but they don't tell you what to write. In Needs they explain how to do everything.

I stare at the blank page so long I start to get sleepy. Maybe if I go to sleep the answer will come in a dream. Maybe if I go to sleep I'll sleepwalk and write the project, and when I wake up it'll be finished.

Maybe not. The only dreams I ever have are about stuff like car chases, explosions, and people yelling at me.

What would Ota dream about? Escaping. Africa. Chimps. People laughing at him from the other side of the bars.

That's it! I could do Ota Benga's dreams. I could write about that. Mr. Blaylock said we could write anything as long as we tied it to Ota. Ota Benga's dreams. How about that?

Or is that stupid? I can never tell unless somebody tells me if it is.

What would he dream? Dreams are like secrets. Everybody has different secrets. How can I find out his dreams?

20

The last bell rang twenty minutes ago, and all the other kids got to go home. But I have to stick around for extra teaching from Mr. B.

Besides me, there's only two other kids who stay behind for bonus lessons. There's Billy, who's a smart kid but he's still learning English because he's from Korea. And then there's Jackie Williams. I don't know why she stays for more—she already knows everything.

"What's next?" she asks Mr. Blaylock.

"Well, we don't move on to chapter eight until next week."

"I know, but maybe I could start now and figure it out."

He smiles down at her. "You're way ahead of the class already. Did you try those extra problems I gave you?"

I *really* don't get her. I mean, going to school is like going to the dentist, you know they're going to find something wrong with you, and you know it's going to hurt. So you want to get out of there as fast as you can. But here's Jackie, sitting in the dentist's chair asking for more.

When Mr. B. comes over to my desk he helps me out with weather. You'd think weather would be easy. It's raining or it's sunny, what more is there?

A lot more. There's all this stuff about why it rains, where it rains, when it rains. I listen until my brain feels soaked.

"Does it rain in Africa?" I ask.

Mr. B. sits on the desk in front of me, and I can hear it creaking under him.

"Of course," he says. "But there are large desert regions where it can go a whole year without rain."

"How about where Ota Benga lived?"

Mr. Blaylock gets up and goes over to pull down the big map of the world that hangs above the blackboard. "Ota lived in the forest, in the Congo. It's not as dry there as it is in the upper half of Africa."

"So he was like Tarzan, swinging through the trees?"

"Not exactly." Mr. B. smiles. "He mostly stayed on the ground. Ota was a great hunter. With his lance—that's kind of like a spear—and bow and arrows he hunted elephants."

"But he was so short, and elephants are huge."

"Well, he worked hard at it, sometimes following

one elephant for days. He would give it these small, stabbing wounds and keep tracking the animal until it bled to death. The elephant was a great spirit to Ota Benga. In his people's songs they would call him Father Elephant. So Ota Benga was surprised when he was brought to the Bronx Zoo and saw a small herd of elephants there."

"Did Ota ever go back home again, to the Congo?"

"A group of African American ministers from churches in New York forced the zoo to let Ota Benga go."

I felt like cheering. Now Ota was free and he could escape back to Africa.

"Then he went to school for a while in America and worked in a tobacco factory. He was homesick a lot of the time, and he died before he could ever get back to Africa."

That's not right. That's not how the story is supposed to end. He has to go back home, to the hot sun and the forest and all the wild animals he loved so much. He can't just die.

"That's a bad ending," I tell Mr. B.

He nods. "Yeah, it sure is. You know, there's an old story from the times of slavery. A priest once asked a dying slave where he thought he was going to go after he died. And the slave said he was going back to Africa. That was his heaven. And maybe that's where Ota Benga's spirit went too. That's what I like to think."

Mr. Blaylock stands up and goes over to check on Billy, who's trying to figure out punctuation.

In my workbook, I turn from my notes on storms and hurricanes to the page where I've got OTA BENGA'S DREAMS underlined at the top and nothing written under it. Just blank paper. I don't even have a first sentence yet.

I've got my great idea, but I don't know what to do with it. How am I supposed to find out what he dreamed?

When Mr. B. is done helping Billy and checks in on Jackie, I stick my hand up.

"Um. For the subject of the project, you said we could write about anything, so long as we tie it to Ota Benga?"

"Right. So what's your idea?" he asks.

"I was thinking maybe I could try and do his dreams as my subject."

I wait to see if he's going to shake his head or tell me I'm an idiot. He rubs his hands together, wiping off chalk dust.

"Interesting," he says finally.

Interesting is way better than *stupid*.

I clear my throat. "I was going to ask you, how do I find that out? It's not in the sheets."

Mr. Blaylock smiles, I'm not sure why. "No, it's not in the sheets. It's not anywhere."

Oh. Great. "So then I guess I can't do that subject?"

He rubs his chin like he's thinking. "Sure you can.

Since he's gone we can't ever know the absolute truth. But if you read up on him, about the Congo and the zoo, I think you could make an educated guess. That's the best anyone could do. If you get in trouble, just put yourself in his place. What if they took you and put you in a zoo, thousands of miles from home? And remember, as strange as he looked to the people who came to see him in his cage, those people looked just as strange to him."

"So I'm just supposed to make it up?" I ask. In school you have the right answer or the wrong one. Making up your own answer is like against the law.

Mr. Blaylock smiles again. "Use your imagination. Ask yourself how you would feel. It's probably not too far from what Ota felt."

Me in the zoo. I stare at the blank page under OTA BENGA'S DREAMS.

21

Sitting at my desk in my room, with papers all over the place and books open to pictures of chimps and orangutans and photos of the Congo, I feel a spark. I'm thinking about teeth. Sharp, pointed teeth. Ota Benga's teeth.

People paid a dime just to see him show his teeth. They laughed and took photos. To them, he must have looked like some kind of vampire. But that was just the way his tribe did their teeth. The Pygmies liked the way it looked. Ota's smile shocked everybody at the zoo. But back home in the Congo, his smile was an everyday, normal sort of smile.

Ota must have thought how weird we looked with our big square teeth. Maybe they looked just as scary to him as his pointy ones did to us.

I pick up my pencil and draw some round faces

with big fat smiles. I try making the smiles wider so the faces are all teeth and the eyes small, black and mean.

When Ota Benga dreamed at night, sleeping in his hammock in the monkey house, I think he probably had a lot of nightmares. I mean, what with all those people laughing at him all day, poking him, chasing and tripping him. I think all the bad things from the daytime would probably get into his dreams at night.

I draw more smiles with fat square teeth. The eyes are tiny and dark like a bat's. And I make the bodies really tall, because Americans must have seemed huge to him. I get out my ruler and add sky-scraping buildings in the background.

It's really starting to look like a nightmare. I just have to color it in some more.

But after this, I have to write *two* whole pages of words besides the drawing. That's the hard part. Reading two pages isn't so bad. I can do that. But putting words together into neat sentences with commas and periods and everything is tough stuff. I remember what Miss Wisswell said about those fat books in the library, how somebody wrote them one word at a time, just like I write one at a time. It's not impossible, but it's sure going to hurt.

When I take a break, I look up at the pictures of Ota Benga on the wall above my desk. There he is, standing in a sunny field holding Polly the chimp. That was like a hundred years ago.

It's just like old reruns on TV, where everybody who's gotten old in the real world is still young. Even though Ota is dead now, he looks so alive in the photo with Polly. He's so far away from where I am, in miles and in years, but I think I can almost feel how sad he is, standing there waiting for them to take his picture.

22

Dad fires up the barbecue and tosses some steaks on. Most people only barbecue in the summer, but Dad loves the burned taste it gives the meat. So even in January sometimes, with the ground covered in snow, he'll be out there in his winter coat flipping burgers.

Right now it's only October, and you can still go outside in just a sweatshirt. Me, I don't mind the cold so much. I mean, look at me—I'm eating a Fudgesicle, watching Dad burn the steaks.

"How do you want yours?" Dad asks me. It's an old joke, because he only cooks them one way.

"Well done," I tell him.

"That's my kid," he says.

"Todd," Mom calls out the back door. "I'm making up some green juice. You want some?"

"No," I say. "I'm off that stuff."

"Really?" she says. "I thought you said it was brain food."

"Yeah. But I drank a whole bunch and ate all those bananas and I never got any smarter."

"Okay, but it's going to be yummy," she says, closing the door.

Yummy if you're a frog, maybe. I should have known that Pond Juice wasn't going to work. I mean, frogs eat that stuff all day long and when was the last time a frog invented something?

I know what Mr. B. would tell me, like when I asked him if there was an easy way to learn fractions.

"There are no shortcuts," he told me. "The only thing that works is hard work."

I take a bite of my Fudgesicle. The cold makes my teeth hurt.

A cool autumn wind stirs the leaves. I stand close to the barbecue to keep warm, but it's melting my Fudgesicle fast. I'm staring into the fire and the crackling coals, thinking about how Ota Benga would cook those elephants his tribe hunted—you'd need one huge barbecue—when Dad shouts:

"Watch out!"

I'm so shocked I drop my Fudgesicle and hold my hand up like somebody's going to hit me. Dad smacks my left arm a few times and I sort of squeeze my eyes shut, like when Zero throws a punch at me.

"You okay?" Dad asks.

I open one eye and nod.

"Don't stand so close to the fire. You got some ash on you there."

I look down at my arm and see a little black burn hole in my sweatshirt. I pull up the sleeve, but the ash didn't get to my skin.

"What's wrong?" Dad says. "You act like I'm going to hit you or something."

I look at my Fudgesicle, where it's lying dead in the grass.

"It's just the yelling and shouting," I say. "Everybody's always yelling at me."

"Don't be scared," he tells me. "I was just born loud. Like my dad. Like Christie. She's like me— she's got no volume control in her brain. You have to grow a thicker skin so it doesn't bother you so much. Be like an armadillo. You know, they're those football-sized animals that look like little tanks. They've got skin like armor. Nobody gets to them."

I lick a drop of Fudgesicle off my arm. Sometimes Dad tells me stuff that never works for me. I mean, what am I supposed to do, walk around wearing a helmet like an armadillo so no one can get to me? I'm never going to have skin like a tank.

And I'm never going to get used to all the yelling. Maybe I *should* go back to Needs. Nobody ever yells there.

23

OTA BENGA'S DREAMS
by Todd Foster
Fifth Grade

At first I thought Ota Benga would dream about his life in Africa. Maybe he would dream about an elephant hunt, or swimming in the river near hippos, or just running under the hot African sun.

And maybe he did dream about that stuff, about good times and all the best places.

But I think that being far away from home in a strange place like the Bronx Zoo where everything is too big and noisy, and everybody is too tall and mean and always bothering you, laughing and chasing you, I think that would give you nightmares.

Where Ota Benga came from, people were short and

had sharp pointy teeth. In New York everybody was tall and had big square teeth, very scary to him.

He must have had nightmares of being stared at and laughed at by these strange-looking crowds, always watching him in his cage. His memories of the Congo must have seemed like dreams too.

I hope he had some good dreams mixed in with the bad ones. But a nightmare was all I could think up.

24

Tuesday morning. History hour.

Mr. Blaylock opens his briefcase and takes out a stack of papers.

"I have your projects here to give back to you," he says.

I feel a shiver like a spider running up my back. This is it! My Mission Impossible.

Mr. B. holds up a page to show the class.

It's a drawing.

It's my drawing—the one I did of Ota Benga's nightmare.

Oh, no. That's it. He's going to fail me all the way back to kindergarten.

"This is amazing," Mr. Blaylock says. "This is a drawing of what Ota Benga might have dreamed in his hammock in the monkey house. It's not a good dream of his African homeland. It's a nightmare, made up of the bits and pieces of his life in this new world he found himself in called America. In the new world everybody was very tall. He was poked and chased and laughed at."

Mr. Blaylock points at stuff in the drawing. "See these faces with the big, frightening smiles? That's how Ota Benga must have seen the crowds that stared at him through the bars of his cage. Look at the small black eyes on those faces. And they have big white teeth, not the sharp pointy teeth of his people back in the Congo. Excellent.

"Todd Foster," he says. "Here's your project back."

I've been holding my breath for over a minute, ever since he held my picture up. Finally I let my breath out and walk up to his desk like my legs are made of Jell-O. I make it there and back without tripping and collapse in my chair.

In the top right corner of my project there's a circle drawn in red marker.

Inside the circle it says B+.

That's impossible!

But it says my name at the top of the paper.

Mr. Blaylock calls out names and everybody goes up and gets their projects. Jackie Williams sits down at her desk. I peek at her paper. A-. Wow, I was only half a letter away from doing as good as her.

I get this weird feeling, I don't know what. I can't say how it feels, except that it's like not being laughed at. It's a new thing. My real name was said out loud in class today. Not Gump or Retardo. It sounds stupid, but it's like I didn't have a real name until Mr. Blaylock called it out just now. Todd Foster.

If this was my old classroom, Eva would be sitting beside me. She'd tell me to pass my project over so she could see. Then she'd trace the B+ with her finger and smell it. The markers she uses all smell like fruits. Eva would be all excited for me and reach over to hold my hand.

The rest of the day is kind of blurry. Mr. B. talks about something called the equator that goes around the world's waist like a belt. I'm going to have to figure that out later, because right now all I can think is B+B+B+B+B+B+B+B+.

After the final bell rings there's just me and Billy left over for extra teaching. When Mr. B. comes over I have to ask him, "Is this right? I never got a B-plus before."

"Well, I'm sure it won't be your last," he says. "Your spelling and sentence structure have really improved. But what impressed me most was your imagination."

I scratch my nose with the eraser end of my pencil. "Making things up never got me anywhere before."

Mr. B. sits on the desk in front of mine, making it groan under his weight.

"Have you ever heard of a man named Albert Einstein?" he asks.

I tap my pencil against my forehead like I'm knocking on it and hoping for an answer. "Was he in the Civil War?"

He smiles. "No. He was a famous scientist in the last century, one of the smartest guys who ever lived. He once said 'Imagination is more important than knowledge.'"

He gives me a few seconds, I guess to let that sink in. I try and figure it out.

Then he goes, "That doesn't mean you don't have to study and know things like fractions and Fahrenheit, longitude and latitude. But it does mean your ideas are important. Nothing new is ever invented without somebody imagining it first."

Mr. B. stands up and says, "Now, was there anything we covered today you didn't understand?"

Later I'm going to have to ask him again what that Einstein guy said, so I can write it down.

But right now there's something else I want to know.

"Yeah," I say. "What's an equator?"

106

25

When I get home, Mom's so thrilled by my B+ she wants to frame it and put it on the wall.

"Pretty gruesome," Christie says when she sees my picture of Ota's nightmare. I think that means she likes it.

Dad tells me, "Knew you could do it, Shaggy." He's calling me that because my hair is the longest it's ever been. I don't look like I'm in the army anymore.

In my room I hold the paper up to my nose and sniff the B+. If it was done with one of Eva's red markers it would smell like strawberry. This one just smells like paper.

It's weird showing my project to everybody. I usually try and hide them when I get them back. It makes my B+ feel real, like it's not just a mistake or something.

But if I could show it to Eva that would make it *really* real, because she'd know how impossible it is to get a B+ in fifth grade. And there's so much stuff I have to tell her—about Ota, and Mr. B., and my new hair. I never even got to tell her about what happened to Psycho.

I go to the kitchen and stare at the phone on the wall. Why doesn't Eva call now? If the phone rings, I'll answer it. We can talk and I won't hang up, and I won't yell at her or anything. I try and force it to ring just by thinking at it real hard. Then I check to make sure it's still working.

It is. But I don't think Eva's going to be calling again, not after I kind of hung up on her, and said no to her party, and acted like a big huge jerk.

She's the one I really want to talk to. But she's the only one I can't talk to.

Now that's dumb!

26

When the bell rings, ending the school day, everybody makes a break for the door. You'd think there was a fire or something the way they're running.

But it *is* Friday.

And I have a plan. I thought it up at breakfast, between Froot Loops, orange juice, and Christie flicking my ears. It goes like this.

The other kids clear out of here fast on Fridays. But I know one kid who takes forever getting all her junk together before she leaves. Eva carries more stuff around than a mountain climber. So I figure I can wait and there'll be nobody left in the halls when I sneak over to Needs to see her. Because I was thinking, who would even know if I hung out with Eva when we're not at school? Or if I went to her party? I mean, it's not like any kids from my class are going to be there. It could be a big secret.

I take my time packing my homework. There's no after-school class with Mr. B. on Fridays.

"How is *Charlotte's Web* coming along?" he asks me.

Everybody else finished reading it a week ago, but he's giving me extra time.

"I'm this close to the end." I show him my thumb and finger almost touching, with room for maybe ten pages. "Is there a happy ending?"

"Well, happy and sad," he says, stuffing papers into his briefcase. "If you're done with the book by Monday we'll compare notes and see what you think."

Comparing notes with Mr. B. about a book, that just blows me away. That's what smart people do, talk about books and stuff.

I say bye and walk out into the hall. There's only a few kids left and most of them are leaving. After taking a long drink at the water fountain and making sure the coast is clear, I go around the corner.

Then I stop dead in my tracks.

Zero and one of his friends are standing by the Special Needs classroom, looking through the window in the door. Zero taps on the glass like it's an aquarium and he's trying to scare the fish.

I freeze up. My whole plan crashes and burns in front of my eyes. I wanted to see Eva in secret. What do I do now?

I could just leave, but I'd have to walk by those two to get to the stairs.

"That's the idiot who's always kissing things," Zero says, staring through the window. "Look at him. He's waving to us."

He's talking about Harvey, who hasn't figured out yet that not everybody's his friend.

Their backs are turned to me right now, and the stairs are maybe fifteen feet away. I could be gone before they even knew I was here.

But I really wanted to tell Eva stuff. I can't go without talking to her anymore. My face is sweating up and my back is shivering at the same time.

"Look at his girlfriend there. What's with the glasses? She thinks she's a model or something."

My heart feels like it's trying to punch its way out of my chest. This wasn't in the plan. But I can't just leave Eva here with those two.

I came to see her. And who cares who knows anymore?

So I take a deep breath and move fast.

"Coming through," I say, squeezing past them to open the door. I get inside before they can take a swipe at me. I slam the door and jump at the noise it makes.

After a second I can breathe again.

"Hey, it's Todd," Harvey shouts, and comes rushing over to me.

Him and Eva are cleaning paint off brushes and rinsing out jars. I go over to the sinks. Harv comes up to me, and I know he's going to try and plant a kiss on me.

"No way, Harv," I say. "If you gotta kiss something, kiss the book."

I hold up my copy of *Science Made Simple* and he gives it a smooch. Why he has to do that all the time, I don't know. Miss Wisswell says it's his way of shaking hands and making friends with everything. Nobody wants Harvey germs, but sometimes they let him kiss their arm or something.

Harvey scratches his chin and smears it with purple from his hand. "Miss Wisswell had to go wash off her shirt, because one of the paint tubes exploded on her."

"It only exploded because you squeezed it so hard," Eva says. She's over by the sink, rinsing brushes.

It's weird being back here. The walls are covered with art, and I can spot a painting I did last year of the class lizard. It's taped right above his terrarium. In the picture I have him eating a big black cricket. Those are his favorite. It's weird seeing my old desk with somebody else's stuff on it.

And it's weird that Eva hasn't even said hi to me yet. She's got her back turned to us, using the sponge to wipe a bottle clean.

I can hear someone outside the door shout, "Gump!" But I don't bother looking.

"So, Eva. Whatcha doing?" It's a stupid question,

but she won't even look at me so I don't know what else to say.

"Washing."

"Need some help?" I ask.

"That's what Harvey's here for."

I look over at Harv, who's trying to squeeze paint back into a tube. And that won't work, unless you've got some kind of superpowers.

"I don't think Harvey's helping much," I say.

"Me neither." Eva puts a clean bottle back on the shelf. "But at least he never yells at me."

"I know. I'm sorry about that. It was just . . . um . . ." I was going to tell her why I had to be like that, what the reasons were. But when I think about them, they're not really good reasons. There's no really good reason to yell at Eva.

"Can I still come to your party?" I ask.

When she turns around I see she's wearing her blue glasses, the ones that make you see things like they're underwater.

She tries to hold her serious face at me, like she's mad, but after a second her smile breaks through.

"Yeah, I guess," she says. "But I'm going to want two presents because of you not calling me."

I hear the door open behind me and I can't help jumping a little. Zero and his friends are coming in. I spin around.

But all I see is Miss Wisswell walking into the room.

"Hello, Todd," she says. "Come back to visit?"

I nod. Miss Wisswell is my all-time favorite teacher. Mr. B. comes in second, only because he doesn't smile so much. Miss W. has an easy smile she gives out all the time.

"Now, Harvey, are you cleaning up or messing up?" she asks him.

Harv has to think about that a minute. "I don't know. Both, I guess," he says finally.

She runs a paper towel under the tap and hands it to him. "It's getting late. I think your mothers are all probably waiting outside. Thanks for helping clean up."

Eva gets together some books from her desk but has to dig through a pile of junk to get to them. She collects everything. You should see her room. It looks like an explosion at a junk factory.

Miss W. helps Harvey get his backpack on. He's looking at all Eva's stuff.

"Can I try on one of your glasses?" Harv asks.

She's got two pairs she was keeping in her desk, plus the blue pair she's got on.

"I don't know," she says. "Are your hands clean?"

He throws them in the air like this is a stickup.

"You better not break them, and don't smudge up the lenses. And you can't take them home."

"Yeah. Yeah. Can I wear the purple ones?" he asks.

"They're called violet." Eva really knows her colors.

Harv tries them on. "Wow. It's like grape juice."

Before we leave the room, I stick my head out. "Okay. It's safe."

We go down the stairs and outside. Harvey's looking around at stuff like he's seeing it for the first time.

"You look like a purple alien," Harv says. "What do I look like?"

"I don't know," I tell him. "An orangutan?"

He loves that so much he starts hooting like a monkey.

I shake my head and look around to make sure nobody's watching. I should tell Harv about Dohong, the orangutan escape artist. He'd love that. And I have to tell Eva about my B+ and Ota Benga.

I think maybe if Ota was still around he could hang out with me and Eva. Harvey could come too. He could hold hands with Dohong.

27

Dad drives me over to Eva's place.

"I'm just going to drop in and say hi," Dad says. "Then you can call me later to come pick you up."

Dad's not big on parties, unless they have green beer like on St. Patrick's Day.

Eva's mom answers the door.

"Hello, Todd," she says. "Haven't seen you in ages. Come on in. The party's out back."

We don't get five steps into the house before Harvey shows up. "Hey, Todd, there's three kinds of cake," he tells me. And it looks like he's got all three kinds smeared on his face. "Who's that?" he asks, looking over at Dad.

I tell him and he goes up and says, "Hi, Todd's dad." Then Harv reaches out and uses both his hands to shake one of Dad's.

"Todd's here. Todd's here," Eva squeals, rushing up to me. She's wearing a tie-dyed T-shirt with crazy swirls of color, one of those shirts that look like a rainbow just threw up on it. And she's got on raspberry-colored glasses.

"I was waiting for you to start the karaoke," she says, handing me and Dad a couple of those party favors that you blow on and they uncurl, making a loud honk. "Hold on, we gotta takes pictures. Mom, where's the camera?"

Eva runs off to find it.

"Okay. Okay." Eva runs back to us. "I've got the camera. I want a picture of you, um, arriving. So stand by the door like you just got here." She points where we should stand. "Okay. And you have to blow on the favors."

I'm used to her trying to take charge and tell me what to do, but it's funny to see her ordering Dad around too. She finally gets us both blowing at the same time and takes a shot on her Polaroid.

"Are you going to stay, Mr. Foster?" Eva asks Dad. Then before he can even answer she says, "You have to eat some cake."

"I don't know. I have to go and . . . ," he starts to tell her, but Eva's smiling like crazy and holding on to his sleeve like she's not going to let him get out of here until he eats something. "Sure. I'll stay. Which way to the cake?"

I wave the instant photo around in the air until it dries. There's me and Dad standing at the door, blowing our favors together. It's a good picture because Dad really looks like Dad, a little bit grumpy, and you can see him clear without any cigarette smoke.

"Come on," Eva says. "The karaoke machine is all set up."

She pulls me out to the backyard. It's still Indian summer outside, so it's real nice and the only way you can tell it's not summer anymore is by all the orange leaves the wind is blowing off the trees.

"I've got a lot of new songs since last time," Eva tells me.

The karaoke machine has speakers and a small TV screen where the words to your song show up so you can sing along to the music. She shows me the list of the songs she has.

"How about this one?" I ask.

"The dog song? We've done that a million times."

"That's because it's the most fun," I say. "And you always like the barking part."

"Let me punch it up." Eva hits the right keys. "Okay. Testing. Testing." She tries out the microphone. The volume is set on the max, so her voice booms over the backyard, and I swear it knocks some leaves off the trees. Now we've got everybody's attention.

"Ooops," she says, turning it down. "Are you ready?" she asks me.

"Ready."

Eva grabs something from her pocket. "You have to wear these."

She holds out a pair of orange-colored glasses. I guess I'm making a face, because then she tells me, "You have to wear them. It's my birthday."

I take the glasses from her and put them on.

"Happy birthday," I say.

Eva has this huge smile on her face. It's crazy how happy this makes her. It's even crazier how happy it makes me.

I forgot how strange everything looks through orange-vision. Doesn't matter what time of day it is, when you look at the sky with orange eyes it always looks like a sunset.

She presses Play on the karaoke machine. There's only one microphone, so we have to share it. Some familiar music starts up.

It's one of our favorite songs, "Who Let the Dogs Out?"

Me and Eva start singing and barking. We sound great, even when we get the words wrong.